The Song of the Pirate Queen

For Scarlet

The Song of the Pirate Queen

Matthew Stringer

© Matthew Stringer 2020

ISBN 9798614245078

Contents

Foreword   vii

The Song of the Pirate Queen   1

Endnotes   41

The Song of the Pirate Queen

Foreword

Among the treasures of the library of the late George Lewis Quain was discovered a volume of the *Encyclopædia of Tlön*. Between the pages of this otherwise unknown work had been secreted, on both sides of a single sheet of foolscap folio, in a neat, minuscule, cursive hand quite distinct from Quain's own, a poem of some 133 quatrains titled *The Song of the Pirate Queen*. It was unsigned. I asked if I might have it: deeming it to be of little interest, his executors allowed this. I apparently thus rescued it from oblivion, as the volume of the *Encyclopædia* cannot now be located.

The Song of the Pirate Queen is a ballad of the high seas, in form somewhat in imitation of Coleridge's *Rime of the Ancient Mariner*, in content seemingly a prequel to Robert Louis Stevenson's *Treasure Island*: mentioned in passing are the characters Ben Gunn, Billy Bones and a Joseph - later perhaps Captain - Flint, as well as a suggested source for Flint's buried treasure. As with Stevenson's inclusion of Israel Hands, it also incorporates a character historically attested in Captain Charles Johnson's *General History of the Pyrates*: here it is Anne Bonny, supposed to have outlived her partner - in crime and in love - John 'Calico Jack' Rackham, who, unlike Bonny, is known to have died on the gallows in 1720. Charles Johnson is furthermore asserted to have been a pseudonym of Daniel Defoe.

The poem is amateur, whimsical and eccentric, perhaps even perverse in its insistence on rhyming every one of its 266 trimeter lines. Even allowing for the use of part-rhymes, this inevitably requires the employment of a significant number of obscure or archaic words. There are, additionally, several classical, literary, historical and mythological allusions. For these reasons I have included endnotes to assist the modern reader's comprehension.

At the suggestion of Mr. A.J.D. Richmond I have also created a series of illustrations to accompany the text. I assert my copyright over these, my endnotes, and, as it is otherwise unattributed, the poem itself.

Matthew Stringer
Aberdeen, February 2020

The Song of the Pirate Queen

The Song of the Pirate Queen

Would you hear a tale of sea and sail
A song of a pirate queen
Who was brave and bold in days of old
And hailed from Aberdeen?

'Tis a rare report, of a finer sort
Than are commonly heard or seen
On the radio, or a TV show
Or cinema's silver screen.

My trade I've plied on the ocean wide
From th' archipelago Philippine
To the isles of spice and the Arctic ice
And everywhere in between.

It was years now past, from a man downcast
Dog drunk in some dour canteen
At a river's mouth on the distant south
Of the shore of the Argentine

That first I heard, though slow and slurred,
The song of the pirate queen
And might I say I had to pay
A flagon of cheap poteen.

Now when I arrived at that fateful dive
He was holding forth, mid-scene
To a few who'd hear, for a wine or beer
A yarn of the high marine

And on he railed of some cursèd whale
Of a whiteness quite obscene
As he quaffed his ale, "call me Ishmael!"
He cried out in between.

He was holding forth mid-scene

The Song of the Pirate Queen

In time he saw that he needed more
Than this tedious old routine:
If his crowd would stay - and for drinks would pay -
He would have to keep them keen

So his beer he downed then he looked around
Sat a moment quite serene
Belched three times, then began the rhymes
Of the song of the pirate queen.

"There's few as knows how this story goes
For this reason: those who've seen
In general - well - don't live to tell
Of the terrible pirate queen.

It's something near three hundred year
Since a girl called Mary Jean
Left a life unsafe as an orphaned waif
In the town of Aberdeen.

Her days were cruel in the poorhouse school
And so our Mary Jean
Ran off to sea in twenty-three
At the age of just thirteen.

Her yellow hair she cropped quite bare
Her limbs were strong and lean
And all who saw her took her for
A cabin boy named Ian.

She made so bold as to be enrolled
In the crew of one Captain Skene
Bound, they say, for Chesapeake Bay
On his ship the *Duncin Sheen*.

She made so bold as to be enrolled

Rigged fore and aft with staysail and gaff
And a hull like a sleek sardine
Was this schooner fair on which Mary dared
Escape from Aberdeen.

The seagulls cried in a cloudless sky
On a north wind fresh and keen
As ropes were hauled and orders called
By the men of the *Duncin Sheen*.

In a little while past the Scilly Isles
And into the wide marine
She sailed on true, with among her crew
The youngster they called Ian.

On she pressed, sailing to the west
Can your mind's eye conjure the scene:
The sunshine bright, the wave-foam white
And the deep of the sea jade-green?

Now I can't tell if you've travelled well;
To the Calms of Cancer been
Where the breezes fail to fill the sail
But that now becomes our scene.

No breath would blow, so they drifted slow
On flat calm aquamarine
For several days in the hot sun's haze
Of those latitudes serene.

So that she might learn Mary took her turn
As the Captain's apprentice keen
And all the arts of reading charts
Were shown to Mary Jean.

The sunshine bright, the wave-foam white

The Song of the Pirate Queen

By quadrant, backstaff, almanac
The longitude to glean
Though this was yore, and years before
John Harrison's machine.

To read the sky, demystify
The motions empyrean
Of Pleiades and Hyades
She learned from Captain Skene.

Though poor winds blew, the Captain knew
Of horse-currents all unseen
Which, while not strong, still moved along
To westward the *Duncin Sheen*.

One day was spied off the starboard side
A speck on the silvered sheen
And all could hear, quite faint but clear
A melody pure and clean.

The spellbound men sprang to action then
And none would contravene
For that female voice leaves no man a choice:
'Twas the fateful song sirene.

By the sirens' song they were swept along
Though the rocks were clearly seen
And such wind as breathed they skilfully seized
For guiding the *Duncin Sheen*.

By sail fore and aft, by all nautical craft
On the orders of Captain Skene
They steered her straight to her dreadful fate
To the horror of Mary Jean.

The longitude to glean

The Song of the Pirate Queen

The crashing sound as she ran aground
Was abominable and obscene.
Over the side men leapt and died
As they quit the *Duncin Sheen*.

On the empty deck of that sorry wreck
There was only Mary Jean.
Then the splintered craft started sinking aft
And to starboard did careen.

Up came the sharks from the watery dark:
Can you picture the awful scene
Of the gaping maws and snapping jaws
Which would make her their cuisine?

But as her doom below her loomed
Just then our Mary Jean
Escaped the deep with a mighty leap
Like a Mexican jumping bean!

By the skin of her teeth she gained the reef.
She turned to survey the scene
And all around had been driven aground
The stuff the ship had been.

This flotsam told her to be bold:
The sails of *serge de Nîmes*
And planks and rope embodied hope
She would not have foreseen.

Our heroine can now begin
To whet her talents keen:
She makes a craft, a simple raft
And rigged as a lateen.

Escaped the deep with a mighty leap

The Song of the Pirate Queen

To keep her fed she had dry bread
Made from garbanzo bean;
One cask, unburst, to quench her thirst
Of wine from the Aegean.

The stars abet and her course is set
By motions empyrean
Of Pleiades and Hyades
Towards the Caribbean.

For several days in the hot sun's haze
On flat calm aquamarine
She drifted slow as no wind would blow
At those latitudes serene.

The implacable sky was set on high;
Far below roamed the great baleen
Where the Kraken sleeps in the darkest deeps
Of indifferent, vast blue-green.

The hopeful sharks in the watery dark
Were all the life to be seen;
All that wet her lips were infrequent sips
Of that wine from the Aegean.

When the wind came at last it was as a storm-blast
And the swell rose cyclopean.
She bound herself fast to the sturdy mast
And struck down the *serge de Nîmes*.

As the tempest raged Mary calmly gauged
How fleeting her life had been:
Would she die alone before she'd grown
A mere girl not yet fourteen?

She bound herself fast to the sturdy mast

'Twas not to be: the Lord calmed the sea
To spare his Mary Jean
And this he crowned by having her found:
By Him are all things foreseen.

A ship drew near and pulled her clear
Of the raft which her saviour had been,
But the men that she faced were a ragged disgrace
Next to those of the *Duncin Sheen*.

Now first she asked them for a flask
Of water fresh and clean;
She slaked her thirst 'til fit to burst
Her stomach or her spleen.

The castaway, I've heard men say
Does not miss *haute cuisine*
Nor does he pine for Bordeaux wine
Nor bacon, fat or lean.

"Oh please appease my need for cheese!"
They asked what might she mean?
"Some Port Salut, some Stilton Blue
Or Gorgonzola green."

Her heart's desire, it did transpire
Was that miracle of casein
Whose magic strange sees mere cows' milk change
To gold in a clay tureen.

At this did one named Benjamin Gunn
Scoff at Miss Mary Jean,
But God had a plan for that selfsame man
To learn what she might mean.

Oh please appease my need for cheese!

They raked around and at last they found
Some Roquefort, high and keen,
Which she dispatched with a speed unmatched
And a delight most Epicurean.

"What man are you, and from which ship's crew,
And how was it you have been
Cast out adrift to the currents swift?"
Asked one who was lank and lean.

"I alone was spared from the sirens' air
Of the crew of the *Duncin Sheen*
And the reason why is no man am I
For my name it is Mary Jean."

They noted with shock her yellow locks
All matted and unclean.
As they stood aghast through their number passed
A lady of haughty mien.

Her face was framed by hair of flame;
She smiled a smile obscene
For her teeth were lacquered deepest black
Though her laughter trilled oscine.

"I am Anne Bonny, Queen of Piracy
And Curse of the Caribbean!
Be my cabin's guest, come and take your rest,
And wash, and dress, and preen."

To the Captain's cabin for a gab
Went Anne and Mary Jean
Where Mary attested, at Anne's behest
Of her flight from Aberdeen,

I am Anne Bonny, Queen of Piracy

Of the sirens' lay, of her castaway
From the wreck of the *Duncin Sheen*,
And Anne then told our heroine bold
Of the life of a pirate queen.

"Now New Providence Isle had seen no trial,
No law for nearly sixteen
Anarchic years when the buccaneers'
Republic of Pirates she'd been

"With fealty owed to the pirate code
And no other tax or lien
There all grew rich on those treasures which
They got by their rapine:

"Pieces of eight, dubloons by the crate,
And emeralds flashing green,
Sapphires of blue and red rubies too,
Topaz and tourmaline,

"Scarlet beryl, black and white pearls
Iridescent as opaline,
The sweat of the sun, gold, by the ton
And the silver tears of Selene,

"But five years past had seen its last
For the crown did intervene
And o'er the sea for our liberty
Sent a squadron of barquentines.

"'Twas Captain Rogers did dislodge -
Smoke out with his dudeen -
Our corsair sort from Nassau port
Back in the year eighteen.

Pieces of eight, dubloons by the crate

"Condemned we stand in the various lands
Which rule the Caribbean
To the gallows broad, the firing squad
or Madame Guillotine.

"Fair Captain Rackham - Calico Jack -
Did the hangman's noose beseen:
The cruel Jamaican court did take
The life of my libertine.

"As I was with child the court dealt me more mild
When brought before that jackeen
The Governor Lawes, through whose leprous paws
I then slipped away unseen.

"Though he brings me joy, the babe was a boy
And so cannot be pirate queen:
Will you be my own, heir to my throne
The daughter I need, Mary Jean?

"This is no life for a timid wife:
You'll needs be twice as mean
As any male with whom you sail
And have no weakness seen."

No kirk nor king was owed a thing
By the orphan Mary Jean:
To kin of her own the nearest she'd known
Went down with the *Duncin Sheen*,

So starting anew in Anne Bonny's crew
On that sloop named the *Skibereen*
In the wild career of a buccaneer
She became an apprentice keen.

In the wild career of a buccaneer

Now France and England's haughty kings
Drew riches beyond obscene
From sugar cane or gold for Spain
And sale of human beings.

These Bonny saved from being enslaved
And following their freeing
They'd give her thanks and swell the ranks
Who sailed with the pirate queen.

They joined a mob with several slobs,
Some dandies and libertines,
A Turk and a Greek, two Hindus, a Sikh
And a brave of the Na-Dene;

From Jacobites and catamites
The learned and the mean
From every land were drawn that band
Who manned the *Skibereen*.

Amongst the crew were those who knew
Philosophy Chaldean,
By night would pore o'er ancient lore
And secrets Damascene;

Their learning ranged from rote to strange
Of wormwood and ethylene,
And Parsee poems; the weighty tomes
Of Plato and Augustine;

They knew the pyrotechnics of Greek Fire
Quicklime and kerosene
Which burns in water, and they taught
All this to Mary Jean;

By nights would pore o'er ancient lore

'Tis even said that with the dead
She learned how to convene
To conjure sprites and compel wights
To do as she might deem.

The years went past until at last
When Mary was seventeen
Command came down from the English crown
To purge the Caribbean.

Corsairs they drove from every cove
Each harbour and shebeen
Of privateers and buccaneers
The navy wiped them clean.

One day at last it came to pass
That a captain young and keen
Named William Rupert spied the sloop
Which belonged to the pirate queen

Now at his command he had, fully manned
A flotilla of three brigantines
He brought these in range and shots were exchanged
By cannon and culverine.

Three salvos, or four, but I'm certain no more
And the furlong or so in between
Was so thickly choked with billowing smoke
That the enemy couldn't be seen.

Being given the slip by Anne's pirate ship
Because of this powder-smoke screen
Poor Captain Rupert found himself duped
In presuming his foe fled the scene.

A flotilla of three brigantines

For a taper was set to a bellowed jet
Of naphtha and lime Byzantine;
Through the gunsmoke she came, exhaling flame
From the prow of the *Skibereen*

The Greek fire went right through a gun port, set light
To the black powder magazine
And the first ship was doomed: with an almighty boom
She was blasted to mere smithereens

The pirate sloop veered off to starboard, was steered
Alongside the next brigantine
And onto this second ship's forecastle deck
Swarmed a mob led by bold Mary Jean

On the deck of that craft they fought their way aft
With the blades of their cutlasses keen
And, swinging their swords, cried "Pray to the Lord!
Make your peace with the good Nazarene!"

Before such ferocity sailors were lost
Many britches were rendered unclean
They fell to their knees crying out "Spare us please
From such violence internecine!"

The fates had allotted that no pistol-shot
Might injure or kill Mary Jean
But the same was not true for Captain Anne, who
Set her foes on a heading Hadean

The cost of this feat was destruction complete
Of the hull of the *Skibereen*:
A delicate frieze, holed like Swiss cheese
By the guns of the last brigantine.

A mob led by bold Mary Jean

Her gunwales, her masts, and her topsail at last
Disappeared as she sank away clean
Some crewmen were saved, but on top of the waves
There was nothing but foam to be seen.

And so Anne Bonny went under the sea
To be with her lost libertine
Where it's said Billy Bones drinks with old Davy Jones
In the verdure of Fiddler's Green.

The solitary boat which was now left afloat
Was that one captured brigantine
Where the sailors who kneeled were offered a deal
By this she-devil named Mary Jean.

For the odd tot of rum they'd been under the thumb
Of their officers ready and keen
At the drop of a hat with lash or with cat
To lay on a stroke or sixteen.

They considered their plight and offered no fight,
Surrendered to Mary Jean,
And swore to the code with their loyalty owed
To their captain the young pirate queen.

From then on this new captain and crew
Adventured on that brigantine
And marked on her prow a fresh name that now
She would sail as: the *Aberdeen*.

Another thing yet she ordered them: "Let
That ensign not be seen:
Our mast-head high shall show to the sky
The flag of the pirate Queen."

In the verdure of Fiddler's Green

They asked what sign she had in mind
"Is it black or Barbary Green
Some ghoulish work or death's-head smirk
Reminiscent of Halloween?"

To this she said "A flag blood red
The most terrible ever seen
As the Frenchmen say, "La Jolí Rougé"
Pure scarlet's what I mean!

"That's the battle jack, it means "Attack!"
To any by whom it's seen
Let strong men quail and turn quite pale
At my banner incarnadine."

From that time forth, all points South and North
East, West, and each in between
All shipping and trade was rendered dismayed
On sighting the *Aberdeen*.

A freer of slaves, and Queen of the Waves
Was acknowledged our Mary Jean:
Her crew waxed rich on those treasures which
They captured by their rapine.

The sweat of the sun, gold, by the ton
And the silver tears of Selene,
Pieces of eight, dubloons by the crate
And emeralds flashing green,

Sapphires of blue and red rubies too,
Topaz and tourmaline,
Scarlet beryl, black and white pearls
Iridescent as opaline:

As the Frenchmen say, "La Joli Rougé"

The Song of the Pirate Queen

Aberdeen freighted a haul of such weight
That few of her draft-marks were seen,
And silver and gold took the space in the hold
Of their powder and shot magazine.

So they stored some in chests, and barrels the rest
And hid it from any regime
On the shores of Belize all tangled with trees,
Hispaniola so fecund and green,

On islands off Cuba, as far as Aruba
And many a cay in between
They buried their troves in tropical groves
And bays where no human had been.

The last of the boxes was filled and was locked
And was taken ashore by a team
To a tenantless isle which measured a mile
And with scarcely a freshwater stream.

The poor little boat was barely afloat
Taking water when rocking abeam
With the weight of the hoard it carried aboard
And a complement numbered nineteen.

Having made it aground they scouted around
And went through their practised routine:
The island was mapped, and this document capped
With an 'X' for the burial-scene,

But once out at sea it turned out by three
The headcount was found to be lean:
They were missing Ben Gunn, Joseph Flint and a man
Of Knoydart, a known Jacobean.

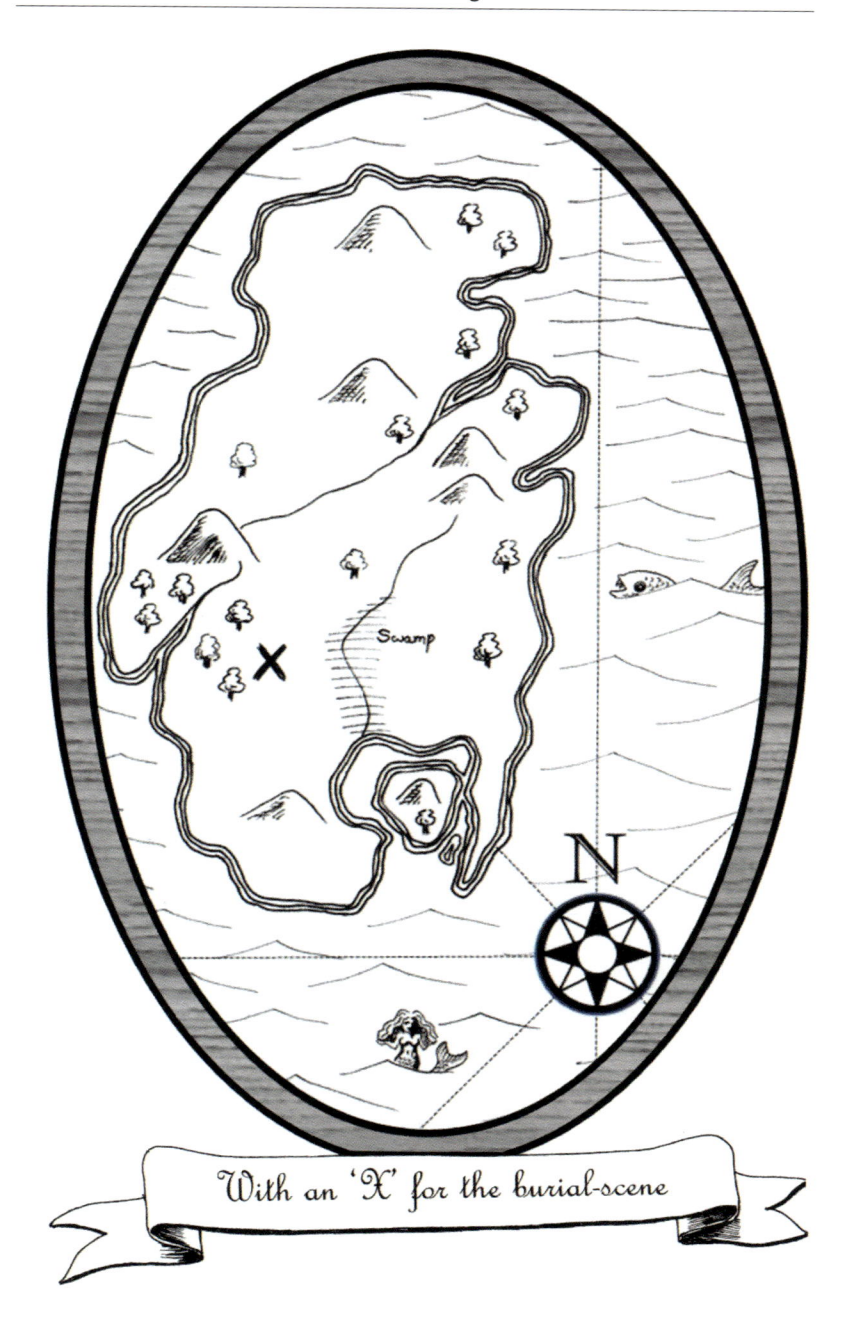

With an 'X' for the burial-scene

They couldn't go back: they fell under attack
From a trio of barquentines
And so this affray left the three castaway
To such fate as God's judgement might deem.

All of this bounty, of such an amount
That Croesus might think it extreme
In jungles and bays remains to this day
Interred in sepulchra unseen.

For a year and a day our Mary held sway
Over all of the wide Caribbean
Until hunting her down was every Crown
Of every land European.

The chase was financed by Spain and by France
And Portuguese House Brigantine;
Though they didn't care much, the Republican Dutch
Sent a handful of ships, to be seen.

The fleet sent by France leaving from Port-au-Prince
Had sighted her making between
The Gulf of Gonâve and a lookout they have
Off Cuba's most eastern extreme,

So knowing she'd take a route past Jamaica -
On a southwestern course she was fleeing -
A cordon of barques formed a huge arc
To the mainland New Andalusian.

All made for the west: French; Spanish; the rest
To trawl for the *Aberdeen*:
The trap being set, they drew in the net
Escaping was just not foreseen,

A cordon of barques formed a huge arc

For the lands held by Spain - the famed Spanish Main -
Circle west of the Caribbean
This landlocking wall offers no way at all
To reach the Pacific serene.

It's no problem today: a canal cuts a way
Through Panama's jungle green
But please don't forget that it wasn't there yet
Having opened in nineteen fourteen.

So rounding Cape Horn - a feat not to be scorned -
Was accepted as fairly routine
Or some would aspire through the Islands of Fire
To pick out a way in between.

Up past Hudson's Bay it was rumoured there may
Be a passage no sailor had seen
Though sagas record not a hint nor a word
That the valiant Vikings had been:

The icebergs and floes do not predispose
Anybody to sail in between
Their hazards in sunlight, and yet for that run
In winter they're even less keen

For up in the Arctic the winter is dark
And the sky dances ghostly and green
With boreal light through six months of night
Over ship-splint'ring frozen marine.

In any event that's not where she went;
She escaped from the Caribbean
By some secret way unknown to this day
Where no other mortals have been.

For up in the arctic the winter is dark

There was no sign she'd drowned, but she couldn't be found;
No trace of her ever was seen
Of the fates of the rest only *Marie Celeste's*
Is as strange as the *Aberdeen*.

Did she sail as far as the baths of the stars
Or into the kingdom of dream?
To the Isles of the Blessed in the utmost west
Where the heroes' repose is serene?

Now Daniel Defoe, of whom you may know,
Pseudonymously, it would seem
Wrote a famed history all about piracy
But failed to include Mary Jean.

He names Captain Bowen and Edward Lowe
Black Roberts and Samuel Keane
And most of the rest of the dispossessed
Who bedevilled the Caribbean;

Old Thomas Tew and Anne Bonny he knew
(Though before she was Pirate Queen)
And he wrote of the feared Edward Teach - Blackbeard -
And considered him shockingly mean,

But not many know how this story goes
For no-one who crossed Mary Jean
Ever lived on to speak so much as a squeak
Of the terrible pirate queen.

So how is it I have somehow survived
To tell you all that I've seen?
That's a separate tale, whose price is an ale
Or a rum, or some other poteen…

Did she sail as far as the baths of the stars?

The Song of the Pirate Queen

Endnotes

Page 2

"the radio, or a TV show" - this provides a *terminus post quem* for the poem's composition in the 1930s, very likely later: it is not ancient, and its internally-presented timeline of transmission is wholly anachronistic.

"curséd whale […] call me Ishmael" - our second narrator presents himself as the narrator of Herman Melville's *Moby Dick*, quoting among the most famous opening lines in literature, and presenting himself as the lone survivor of one of its greatest seafaring adventures. See 'Concluding Remarks' for further discussion.

Page 4

"in twenty-three" - 1723, because "near three hundred" years ago. Given that Mary Jean was thirteen at this time, she must have been born 1709-1710.

"a cabin boy named Ian" - women and girls would not be permitted to join a ship's crew. Such women as went to sea did so by disguising themselves as men.

"the *Duncin Sheen*" - in the 'Doric' Scots of northeastern Scotland the plural of 'shoe' is 'sheen', retaining an older plural form: Captain Skene's ship is the 'Dancing Shoes'

Page 6

"Rigged fore-and-aft with staysail and gaff" - as opposed to square-rigged, this is the usual sailplan of a schooner.

"Calms of Cancer" - also known as the 'horse latitudes', these are the regions roughly at the latitude of the Tropic of Cancer which lie between the westerly winds to the north and the easterlies to the south.

Page 8

"By quadrant, backstaff, almanac / The longitude to glean [...] John Harrison's machine" - prior to the development of reliable marine chronometers (clocks which stayed accurate aboard ships across variations of temperature and humidity, and in the presence of constant motion) by John Harrison in the decades immediately following our story, navigation was significantly more difficult due to the uncertainty in calculating longitude. The quadrant and backstaff both allow the calculation of local time, but comparing this to universal time required checking a large number of other celestial measurements for comparison with the data provided in almanacs for this purpose.

"empyrean" - the highest of the heavenly spheres in the old geocentric Ptolemaic cosmology, here simply used to indicate the apparent motions of the sun, moon and stars.

"Pleiades and Hyades" - constellations, again involved in navigation.

"horse-currents" - Captain Skene makes use of these 'horse currents', connected to the name 'horse latitudes', to keep moving westward despite the lack of wind.

"the fateful song sirene" - in classical mythology (most famously in Homer's *Odyssey*) the beautiful song of the sirens caused all men to make directly towards the rocks from which the monstrous sirens sang, luring them to their death. Mary Jean, being female, is apparently immune. See 'Concluding Remarks' for further discussion.

Page 10

"careen" - of a boat, to lean it over onto its side. This might be done intentionally to maintain or repair the hull, with the same term being applied.

"flotsam" - the term for the wreckage left floating when a ship sinks, often used in conjunction with the 'jetsam' jettisoned in an effort to keep her afloat.

"*serge de Nîmes*" - a cotton cloth made in the southern French town of Nîmes, traditionally used as sailcloth. Today this name is contracted to 'denim'.

"rigged as a lateen" - a sailplan from late classical times; a triangular sail hung from a spar extending fore-and-aft, lower at the front. Today most famously associated with the Arabic *dhow* of the Indian Ocean.

Page 12

"garbanzo bean" - chickpeas, implying the bread is similar to Italian *farinata*.

"wine from the Aegean" - of the islands between the Greek and Turkish mainlands, Chios - birthplace of Homer - was particularly famed in ancient times for the quality of its wines.

"abet" - to help or assist

"the great baleen" - now used to differentiate whales which feed on krill, but in older usage referring to whales in general.

"the Kraken" - a huge sea-monster of Norse mythology.

"cyclopean" - of the Cyclops, the one-eyed giants of classical mythology, most famously Polyphemus in the *Odyssey*. Here the term simply signifies 'huge'.

Page 14

"casein" - the protein in milk which allows cheese to form.

"Benjamin Gunn" - in Robert Louis Stevenson's *Treasure Island*, the protagonist Jim Hawkins meets a castaway named Ben Gunn who has developed an obsessional craving for cheese during his isolation. The events of *Treasure Island* date to around 1754, 31 years after Mary Jean's rescue: it appears that this is the same Ben Gunn as a younger man.

Page 16

"Epicurean" - Epicureanism, named for the philosopher Epicurus, is an ancient philosophy which suggests that meaning in human life is to be found in enjoyment. Its detractors - particularly Christian writers - later portrayed this as an amoral and purposeless pursuit of the pleasures of the flesh, such as gluttony.

"haughty mien" - with an arrogant expression on her face.

"hair of flame" - 'fiery' red hair.

"her teeth were lacquered deepest black" - a practise originating in the Far East, particularly Japan. Before modern dental hygiene it was a method of protecting teeth from decay.

"her laughter trilled oscine" - oscines are songbirds: her laughter sounded like a songbird.

"Anne Bonny" - Anne Bonny was a real person, and the account she gives to Mary Jean of the Pirate Republic at Nassau on New Providence, her lover 'Calico' Jack Rackham being hanged, and her surviving because she was pregnant all fits with what is known from other sources. Her fate after 1720 is not recorded elsewhere.

Page 18

"New Providence Isle" - largest island of the Bahamas.

"Republic of Pirates" - established on New Providence, specifically the city of Nassau, in 1703: following a Spanish attack, the settlement was increasingly occupied by pirates, who eventually organised themselves to live under a version of the 'pirate' code which they were used to at sea. In 1718 the Royal Navy intervened to end it.

"Pieces of eight" - the silver dollars of the Spanish Empire, worth eight *reales*.

"dubloons" - the gold Spanish 'double' escudo, worth thirty-two *reales*.

"Sapphires [...] rubies [...] emeralds [...] topaz [...] tourmaline" - various gemstones. Sapphire and, particularly, emerald mining in what is now Colombia was and remains a significant industry.

"The sweat of the sun, gold" - an Incan terminology for gold. The civilisation of the Incas was the source of a lot of Spanish gold in the late sixteenth century, but of course was South American (rather than Central, as in the case of the Maya and Aztec): the metaphor here is somewhat out of place as well as time.

"the silver tears of Selene" - the Incan partner of the above, 'the tears of the moon' for silver, but here using the name of the moon-goddess of Greek myth. Note that Selene should be pronounced with three syllables: the understandable limits of Anne Bonny's classical education are revealed by her pronunciation.

"barquentine" - a ship of three masts where the foremast is square-rigged but the main and mizzenmast are gaff-rigged.

"dudeen" - a short tobacco pipe made of clay.

Page 20

"Madame Guillotine" - another of our author's anachronisms: while similar devices had been in occasional use in various European countries for centuries prior to 1723, Joseph-Ignace Guillotin, after whom was named the device infamously adopted in 1789 during the French Revolution, would not be born until 1738.

"Captain Rackham – Calico Jack" – John Rackham. Lover of Anne Bonny, who left her husband James Bonny (an employee of Woodes Rogers, governor of the Bahamas) and ran off to sea with Jack. Rackham sailed under a black flag with a skull above crossed cutlasses in white. In October 1720 he was captured when he and his crew were incapacitated through drink.

"beseen" – to array or furnish, here perhaps "decorate".

"The cruel Jamaican Court" – Rackham was hanged in Port Royal (now part of Kingstown), Jamaica in November 1720.

"libertine" – one who spurns accepted morals, a sense of responsibility, or sexual restraints. While the term became popular later in the eighteenth century, it was extant: this is less of an anachronism than some of the other examples herein.

"jackeen" – a rural Irish derogatory term for a Dubliner, or thence city dwellers more generally.

"slipped away unseen" – the fate of Anne Bonny is not recorded, so this escape, not further explained, is the key historical conceit of this work.

"cannot be Pirate Queen" - here Anne suggests that she has formalised the idea of the Pirate Queen aboard her ship: in contradiction of the usual proscription of women on board, she has made the succession of her captaincy exclusively female.

"the *Skibereen*" - a town in County Cork, Ireland, mentioned above as Anne's childhood home, although not Skibereen itself. The precise connection is unknown.

"buccaneer" – a specifically Caribbean term which developed to be synonymous with pirate.

Page 22

"France and England's haughty kings" – Louis XV and George I respectively. George was in fact monarch of Great Britain following the 1707 Act of Union between England and Scotland; even without that union he would have been King of Scotland also. It may be that the choice here to refer to him as King of England is related to the derogatory context by either a speaker with Jacobite leanings or an author with Scottish Nationalist sympathies.

"sugar cane" – this plant was brought to Hispaniola by Christopher Columbus himself, and by the eighteenth century shipping sugar to Europe formed one side of the 'trade triangle': made into rum in Europe, the profits of this bought manufactured goods - thus providing the impetus behind Britain's industrial revolution - which were taken to West Africa to be bartered for the slaves who would in turn be exchanged for molasses in the Caribbean.

"gold for Spain" – the mainlands of Central and South America were under the control of the Iberian kingdoms, predominantly Spain. This led to the gold of the mainland civilisations, especially the Aztecs and the Incas, being taken off to Spain. The privateers of other European nations would endeavour to interrupt this transport.

"sale of human beings" – the transatlantic slave trade, mentioned above as one of the sides of the 'triangle trade'.

"dandies" – another anachronism: this word finds this usage towards the end of the eighteenth century.

"brave of the Na-Dene" – this appears to mean a member of one of the various tribes native to the Pacific Northwest of North America. It is very much a colonialist term rather than the name of any people with whom this individual might self-identify, but then it shares this dubious honour with not only 'Indian', but also 'aboriginal' or 'native American'.

"Jacobites" – a supporter of the claim of 'The Old Pretender' James Francis Edward Stuart, son of King James II and VII who had been deposed by the English government in 1688 in favour of William of Orange, husband to James' daughter Mary, but, crucially, a Protestant in opposition to the Old Pretender's Catholicism. While lowland Scotland was Calvinist, and so significantly further from Catholicism than Anglicanism, the English had unilaterally replaced the King of Scotland, scion of the Scottish House Stuart, and so, especially in the Highlands and western islands of Scotland where Catholicism had not been displaced, the Stuart claim retained support. Of course, being a professed Jacobite constituted treason.

"catamites" – a homosexual, from a corruption of "Ganymede", beloved of Zeus.

"philosophy Chaldean" – Chaldea was the name of southern Mesopotamia in Old Testament times, and the Chaldeans were regarded by their Babylonian conquerors as having great arcane knowledge, as evidenced for example by a Chapter 2 of the *Book of Daniel* which pits Daniel against 'the Chaldeans' in the interpretation of Nebuchadnezzar's dream.

"secrets Damascene" – of Damascus, amongst the oldest cities in the world. As with 'Chaldean', this plays to European ideas of the orient as the home of ancient, occult knowledge.

"wormwood" – plants of the genus Artemisia, used historically in medicines, mentioned in the Bible as a byword for bitterness.

"ethylene" – modern name ethene, the juxtaposition of this modern, scientific substance with the folk-medicine herb of Biblical connotation speaks to the eighteenth century as that of the Enlightenment.

"Parsee poems" – the literature of the Zoroastrians.

"the weighty tomes / of Plato and Augustine" – two important early writers of the Western Canon, Plato of Classical Athens, Augustine of the early Christian Church.

"the pyrotechnics of Greek Fire / Quicklime and kerosene" – "Greek fire" was a weapon of the Byzantine (Eastern Roman) Empire, believed to be principally composed of calcium oxide and liquid hydrocarbons, as suggested here.

Page 24

"with the dead / she learned how to convene" – this casual aside is not made relevant in the rest of the narrative. It plays to European ideas of oriental magic, although is also reminiscent of the *nekyia* in Book 11 of the *Odyssey*.

"when Mary was seventeen" – therefore in 1727.

"corsairs" - the French term for privateers, here synonymous with 'pirate'.

"shebeen" – Irish or Scottish Gaelic: an illicit drinking establishment.

"William Rupert" – otherwise unattested.

"brigantines" – a two-masted ship, square-rigged on the foremast and commonly with square topsail on the mainmast, but with a gaff sail below that.

"culverine" – a type of naval gun, smaller than a cannon.

"furlong" – 220 yards, or approximately 200 metres.

"billowing smoke" – gunpowder - 'black powder' - emits a lot of smoke when fired, in contrast to modern ammunition propellants.

Page 26

"naphtha and lime Byzantine" – the 'Greek Fire' mentioned previously is deployed by the crew of the *Skibereen*.

"the good Nazarene" – Jesus 'of Nazareth'.

"a heading Hadean" – towards Hades, the underworld of Greek mythology.

Page 28

"Billy Bones" - one Billy Bones is the 'Captain' from the early part of *Treasure Island* whose arrival at the Admiral Benbow Inn precipitates the whole of Robert Louis Stevenson's adventure. He is a drunkard: given the references already made to Ben Gunn, it seems likely that this reference is to the same character.

"Davy Jones" - 'Davy Jones' Locker' is a nautical idiom for the bottom of the sea. Its origins are unclear, but 'Jones' may derive from the Biblical Jonah through his ordeal in the belly of the whale.

"Fiddler's Green" - a paradisiacal afterlife for sailors drowned at sea.

"the odd tot of rum" - the Royal Navy's 'tot', or ration of alcoholic drink, had been issued in gin since the Anglo-Dutch wars of the seventeenth century, but Caribbean sugar production meant that rum was increasingly given in its place.

"with lash or with cat" - corporal punishment aboard Navy ships would be by the lash, the most infamous form of which was the 'cat of nine tails', here simply the 'cat'.

"swore to the code" - the Pirate Code, in whichever version Mary Jean adopted from Anne Bonny's version.

"ensign" - the national flag flown on a ship to indicate citizenry.

Page 30

"Barbary Green" – the Barbary (Berber) Corsairs of Ottoman North Africa sailed under flags which were often primarily green, which has since been incorporated into the Algerian national flag.

"ghoulish work or death's-head smirk" – variations on the skull-and-crossbones, such as Calico Jack's skull and crossed cutlasses, or skeletons, were popular on pirate flags.

"La Jolí Rougé" – this term, perhaps the origin of the English phrase 'Jolly Roger', in French refers to the "pretty red" flag which, as Mary Jean observes, signalled attack.

Page 32

"draft-marks" – marks on the hull of a boat indicating how low in the water she is sitting due to how much cargo she is carrying.

"Belize" – the area of the eastern coast of the Central American mainland which is the modern country of Belize had not been settled by the Spaniards due its wild nature and the belligerence of the native peoples. The main European interest in the area therefore came from British pirates.

"Hispaniola" – the island which is today divided between the nations of Haiti (from the French colony) in the west and the Dominican Republic (from the Spanish) to the east. Incidentally also the name of the schooner purchased by Squire Trelawney in *Treasure Island*.

"Cuba" - the largest of the Caribbean islands, directly west of Hispaniola, at this time a Spanish colony.

"Aruba" - an island off the north coast of Venezuela, still a Dutch possession.

"cay" – or 'key', a small island formed where a coral reef reaches the sea surface.

"abeam" – horizontally perpendicular to the vessel's long axis, so here indicating the rocking of the boat side to side.

"with an 'X' for the burial-scene" - the idea that 'x marks the spot' on a pirate treasure map was conceived for and popularised by *Treasure Island*.

"Ben Gunn, Joseph Flint" - we have seen already that this is the same Ben Gunn from *Treasure Island*: it is difficult to avoid the further conclusions that "Joseph Flint" is Stevenson's Captain Flint, and also that this is the source of Flint's treasure in Stevenson's story.

"a man / of Knoydart, a known Jacobean" - Knoydart is a peninsula of western Scotland. 'Jacobean' here is presumably simply a variant of Jacobite. Whether this man can be traced, as with his companions, to the pages of *Treasure Island* is unclear.

Page 34

"left the three castaway" - the mechanism by which Ben Gunn and Flint become separated from the Aberdeen in order to later appear in *Treasure Island*.

"Croesus" - a King of Lydia renowned in antiquity for his legendary wealth.

"sepulchra" - a Latinate plural of 'sepulchre'.

"Portuguese House Brigantine" - the House of Braganza, which had ruled Portugal since 1640, was anglicised as the 'Brigantine' dynasty.

"Port-au-Prince" - now capital of Haiti, then the main port of the French colony.

"Gulf of Gonâve" - the Gulf at the western end of Hispaniola on which Port-au-Prince is sited and which opens onto the straits separating Hispaniola from Cuba.

"barques" - a ship of three masts, square-rigged on the foremost two and gaff-rigged on the (aftmost) mizzenmast.

"the mainland New Andalusian" - New Andalusia province was what is now eastern Venezuela, so forming a southern boundary of the eastern edge of the Caribbean.

Page 36

"the Pacific serene" - a tautology. The ocean was so named by Ferdinand Magellan due to the contrast with the experience of rounding Cape Horn to reach it.

"Islands of Fire" - *'Tierra del Fuego'*, the 'Land of Fire', comprises an archipelago off the southern tip of mainland South America. Navigation through the channels so formed offers an alternative to 'rounding the Horn' in the open sea.

"up past Hudson's Bay" - the 'Northwest passage' had been sought as an alternative route between the Atlantic and Pacific, but without success. A key impediment was finding a route not blocked by arctic ice, as discussed in the following stanzas

"valiant Vikings" - in recognition that the Atlantic had been crossed by Leif Erikson centuries before Columbus, and at these intemperate northern latitudes to boot.

Page 38

"*Marie Celeste*" - the ship found drifting and abandoned in the famous historical incident was named the '*Mary Celeste*': the adjustment to '*Marie Celeste*' was made by Arthur Conan Doyle in his short story *J Habakuk Jephson's Statement* which deviated significantly from the historical facts.

"as far as the baths of the stars" - *cf.* Tennyson's *Ulysses* "to sail beyond the sunset / and the baths of all the western stars".

'the Isles of the Blessed' - in Homer these are the Elysian Fields, set across the ocean at the western limit of the world, and populated by warrior heroes and demigod relatives of the immortal Olympians.

'Daniel Defoe' - a trader and prolific writer of the late seventeenth and early eighteenth centuries, today best known as the author of *Robinson Crusoe*. The assertion here is that when *A General History of the Pyrates* was published in 1724, its author, the otherwise unknown Captain Charles Johnson, was in fact a pen-name for Defoe.

'Captain Bowen [...] Edward Lowe [...] Black Roberts [...] Samuel Keane [...] Thomas Tew [...] Edward Teach' - presented as various historical pirates mentioned by Captain Charles Johnson, although note that Samuel Keane appears to be an invention of our poet.

Concluding Remarks

Reflecting on the preceding observations, what might we deduce in respect of our author and his purpose? In my foreword I noted that the poem constituted a prequel to Stevenson's *Treasure Island*, and indeed it conforms to several of the stereotypes of pirate yarns established or popularised by that work. Stevenson's own inspiration, the work of the shadowy Captain Johnson, is also noted.

However, the crew of Stevenson's *Hispaniola* are Englishmen, while the men who crew Bonny's *Skibereen* are drawn from across the world. In this they are more reminiscent of the shipmates of Ishmael in Herman Melville's *Moby Dick*, a novel set a century later, and of far greater geographical scope. Firstly, this poem claims to be the second-hand report of one who cries "call me Ishmael!" as he recounts a tale of a white whale.

In passing it also more resembles Melville's work in a sense of the mythic scale of the ocean under the open sky, mentioning the legendary Kraken alongside the "great baleen" which are the focus of Melville's novel. And, of course, we have a sole survivor of the wrecks of both the *Duncin Sheen* and the *Pequod*.

There is, however, a third literary work allusions to which permeate *The Song of the Pirate Queen*, as they have so many tales of adventure and the seas for twenty-six centuries. It is glimpsed in the encounter with the sirens; in the escape from shipwreck, alone on a simple raft supplied only with bread and wine; in the "cyclopean" swell of the storm; in the passing mention of learning to talk with the dead; in the allusion to Tennyson's *Ulysses* and the Isles of the Blessed as Mary Jean's suggested final destination: that work is, of course, the *Odyssey* of Homer.

Both Mary Jean and Odysseus conceal their identities, both are preternaturally resourceful, brave, and capable of extraordinary feats. Furthermore, and in contrast to either *Treasure Island* or *Moby Dick*, the *Odyssey* is peopled with female characters as well as male: not only Penelope and Helen, but Calypso, Nausicaä, Circe, the Sirens, Scylla and Charibdis. If the later novels were the only model, the female protagonist of *The Song of the Pirate Queen* should seem a more outlandish inclusion than her meeting with the Sirens. It is telling that it is the reality of Anne Bonny's historically attested piratical career which provides the support for an idea so lacking in these fictions. Granted, Homer cannot go so far as to have a female protagonist, but here even the differences are suggestive: a young girl escaping from the constraints of her birthplace is precisely the antithesis of the grown man struggling to return home: can this really be accidental?

There are, additionally, formal similarities. Both are long-form poems rather than prose, although of course the balladic whimsy of *The Song of the Pirate Queen* is not to be found in

Homer's hexameters. Then there is the nested structure of report: our poet quotes 'Ishmael', who apparently knows the details of how Mary Jean alone survived the wreck of the *Duncin Sheen*, who tells tales of sirens and shipwreck to Anne Bonny - just as Odysseus tells the Phaeacians - before, in the middle part of *The Song of the Pirate Queen*, Anne Bonny tells her tale of the Republic of Pirates to Mary Jean.

Granted the scale is utterly different, but these undoubted parallels suggest an author who regarded the *Odyssey* as the progenitor of all the succeeding tall tales of adventure on the high seas, of which *Treasure Island*, *Moby Dick* and this little poem are all examples.

Printed in Poland
by Amazon Fulfillment
Poland Sp. z o.o., Wrocław